BRooklyn

Jacqueline Woodson

illustrated by
Leo Espinosa

The World Belonged to Us

NANCY PAULSEN BOOKS

NANCY PAULSEN BOOKS · An imprint of Penguin Random House LLC, New York
First published in the United States of America by Nancy Paulsen Books, an imprint of Penguin Random House LLC, 2022
Text copyright © 2022 by Jacqueline Woodson · Illustrations copyright © 2022 by Leo Espinosa

Visit us online at penguinrandomhouse.com

Library of Congress Cataloging-in-Publication Data
Names: Woodson, Jacqueline, author. | Espinosa, Leo, illustrator. · Title: The world belonged to us / Jacqueline Woodson; illustrated by Leo Espinosa. · Description: New York: Nancy Paulsen Books, 2022. · Summary: "A group of kids celebrate the joy and freedom of summer on their Brooklyn block"—Provided by publisher. · Identifiers: LCCN 2021032496
ISBN 9780399545498 (hardcover) | ISBN 9780399545528 (ebook) | ISBN 9780399545504 (ebook)
Subjects: CYAC: Summer—Fiction. | Play—Fiction. | Brooklyn (New York, N.Y.)—Fiction. | LCGFT: Picture books.
Classification: LCC PZ7.W868 Wo 2022 | DDC [E]—dc23 · LC record available at https://lccn.loc.gov/2021032496

Manufactured in the USA · ISBN 9780399545498 · 10 9 8 7 6 5 4 3 2 1 · PC

Design by Nicole Rheingans · Text set in Gelica · The art was done with a mighty pencil and Adobe Photoshop.

To young people everywhere.
Keep playing! —J.W.

To my childhood friends.
Tag, you're all it! —L.E.

**In Brooklyn
in the summer
not so long ago**

grown-ups always had someplace to be
or some kind of work to do, but the minute
school ended, us kids were free as air.
Free as sun. Free as summer.

And even before school ended, the street got so hot
that someone always found a wrench
to turn the hydrant on. And someone else
found a soup can to scrape against the curb
till the top and bottom were gone
and it wasn't a soup can anymore.
It was a super shooter!

And our mamas opened the windows and hollered

Don't get your school clothes wet!

But we *had* to run through the water,
bookbags and all. Because our teachers' final words had been

Have a good summer.

Our only plan on that last day of school
was to take what they said seriously.

In Brooklyn
in the summer
not so long ago

my mom would straighten my hair for school
with a hot comb, then twist it into spiraling curls
that she said *Should last awhile.*

But they only lasted until I ran
headfirst into the hydrant,
and quick as that, my hair sprung back
from straightened curls to natural coils

because it was finally summer
and hair too
had a right to be free.

From the end of breakfast till the beginning

of dinner every single day

all summer long

we played in the street

shooting bottle caps we filled with tar

across chalk-drawn skully boards.

We spun tops and learned to take turns
and flicked our double-dutch ropes into blurs, singing

Not last night but the night before
A nickel and a pickle came knocking at my door . . .

And we jumped
and we ran
and we played
and the whole wide world
felt like it belonged to us.

And some days we scraped our knees. But there was always
an older kid nearby who'd say *It's gonna be all right*
and might even tell us stories about being our age,
about stitches and broken arms.
And if someone said *Boys don't cry*, some big boy
always said *Oh yeah?* and had a story
about the time he cried and cried
until our eyes grew wide.
Our hurt knees forgotten.

There was always some new kind of fun.
We built forts out of enormous boxes
then admired what we made together.

We said **You sure can draw**
and **You sure can build**
and **You sure can jump**
and **You sure can sing**

and we meant it.

In Brooklyn
in the summer
not so long ago

it was easy to believe that anything was possible
when a guy from our block was good enough
to play for the Mets and a girl from our block sang
on a big stage in Manhattan and a woman someone's
cousin knew wrote a whole book about Brooklyn.

And someone always had a ball and a stick
to hit it with or a stoop to throw it against.
And if they didn't, we found a soda can and played
steal the bacon and kick the can.

**In Brooklyn
in the summer
not so long ago**

we learned to watch and listen
playing tag, ringolevio, and hide-and-seek
inside hallways and behind thin-limbed trees
and garbage cans.

And our block was the whole wide world
and the world belonged to us.

Afternoons, when we heard the beautiful sound
of an ice cream truck,
we yelled up to our mothers

*Can I have fifty cents
for a cone with rainbow sprinkles?*

And sometimes our mothers wrapped change
into scarves and tossed them down to us.

And our scarves of money held high
became a parade of us kids
chasing a truck with our own song—

Wait! Wait! We want a cone.

Then we shared with the friends with no money
because some days the ones with no money
were us.

In Brooklyn
in the summer
not so long ago

we didn't need doorbells or telephones.
Just two hands to cup around our mouths
and a voice loud enough to be heard.

So we called out to each other

in **Spanish**
in **English**
in **Polish**
in **German**
in **Chinese**

and we ruled
the block in all of our
languages, playing and
playing and playing
until
dusk fell
and the streetlights
came on.

And one by one, our mothers raised
their windows again, this time to call us home.

So we said *To be continued.*

We said *You're still it.*

We said *Don't forget—it was my turn.*

We said *Wear your green T-shirt and I'll wear mine.*

We said *What are you having for dinner?*

Maybe I can eat over tomorrow?

And as our words echoed out over the block
like a lullaby we'd always remember,
I ran up the stairs of my stoop
already excited about tomorrow

and the tomorrow after that
and the many tomorrows to come.

Not just in Brooklyn.

Not just in the summer . . .

but everywhere I'd ever go
and always.